PETER RABBIT ™
TALES
BEATRIX POTTER

She looked suspiciously at the sack and wondered where everybody was?

PETER RABBIT™
TALES

THE ORIGINAL AND AUTHORIZED EDITION BY

BEATRIX POTTER

New colour reproductions

FREDERICK WARNE

The reproductions in this book have been made using the most modern electronic scanning methods from entirely new transparencies of Beatrix Potter's original watercolours. They enable Beatrix Potter's skill as an artist to be appreciated as never before, not even during her own lifetime.

FREDERICK WARNE
Published by the Penguin Group
Penguin Books Ltd, 27 Wrights Lane, London W8 5TZ, England
Penguin Putnam Inc., 375 Hudson Street, New York, NY 10014, USA
Penguin Books Australia Ltd, Ringwood, Victoria, Australia
Penguin Books Canada Ltd, 10 Alcorn Avenue, Toronto, Ontario, Canada M4V 3B2
Penguin Books (N.Z.) Ltd, 182-190 Wairau Road, Auckland 10, New Zealand

Penguin Books Ltd, Registered Offices: Harmondsworth, Middlesex, England

First published in 1998 by Frederick Warne

1 3 5 7 9 10 8 6 4 2

ISBN 0 7232 4483 9

Printed and bound in Great Britain by William Clowes Limited, Beccles and London

CONTENTS

The Story of Beatrix Potter   6

The Tale of Peter Rabbit   19

The Tale of Benjamin Bunny   31

The Tale of The Flopsy Bunnies   47

The Tale of Mr. Tod   59

The Story of A Fierce Bad Rabbit   89

THE STORY OF BEATRIX POTTER

Beatrix, aged 8, with her parents, Rupert and Helen Potter

Beatrix Potter was born in 1866 to Rupert and Helen Potter. She had a conventionally sheltered Victorian childhood and was educated at home by a governess. Beatrix's well-to-do parents disapproved of her forming friendships with children of her own age, so she had a somewhat lonely childhood. Though she was not allowed to mix with her peers, Beatrix met many famous artists, politicians and thinkers when they came to visit her father. For companionship, Beatrix and her younger brother filled the nursery with numerous pets of all varieties. At one stage, the menagerie consisted of a green frog, two lizards, some water newts, a snake and a rabbit, all of which were carefully studied by the children.

From the age of 16 Beatrix Potter took most of her summer holidays in the Lake District with her family. They often stayed on the shores of Derwentwater, a lake popular with many sportsmen, photographers and painters. Beatrix loved Derwentwater from her first visit. She climbed the fells around the lake and went out to the four little islands in the middle. She walked in the woods by the shore, watching the squirrels there, and observed the rabbits in the gardens of the houses where she stayed. She filled little notebooks with her watercolour sketches of the surrounding landscapes. The name of Beatrix Potter is forever associated with the Lake District, and her little books evoke the timeless beauty of the area to millions who have never visited it.

Rupert Potter, a keen amateur photographer, often took pictures of Derwentwater.

From an early age Beatrix drew everything around her, and covered pages with sketches of animals. Her childhood sketchbooks feature fantasy pictures of animals engaged in human activities, such as rabbits ice skating and wearing clothes. With the encouragement of her Uncle Henry, who suggested that she might try selling her drawings, Beatrix began work on six whimsical designs using her pet rabbit as her model. They were bought for £6 by the publisher Hildesheimer & Faulkner, who asked to see more of her work. Beatrix was delighted. Some of the designs were published as Christmas and New Year cards in 1890. At the age of 24, Beatrix had begun her professional career. The earning of her own money was a source of great comfort to Beatrix, who had always dreamed of being independent.

Above, left: Beatrix observed her pet rabbits' behaviour and painted them in different positions.
Above, right: One of Beatrix's Christmas card designs, published in 1870

Noel Moore

Beatrix Potter enjoyed writing letters to children, and it was in these letters that she began to write and illustrate her stories. A picture letter dated 4th September 1893 (see overleaf) was the origin of *The Tale of Peter Rabbit*. The letter was sent to Noel Moore, who was the son of Beatrix's ex-governess, when he was ill in bed. It told the story of a disobedient rabbit named Peter, and it has become one of the most quoted and famous letters ever written. A few years later, it occurred to Beatrix Potter that she might make a little book out of the story. She wrote to ask if Noel had kept the letter, and if so could she borrow it? Noel *had* kept the letter, and was glad to lend it to her.

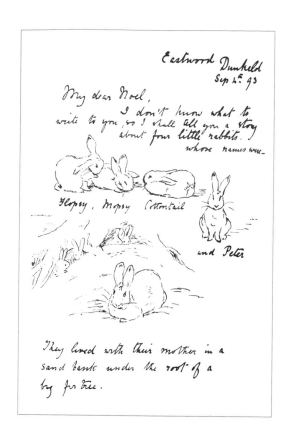

Eastwood Dunkeld
Sep 4th 93

My dear Noel,
    I don't know what to
write to you, so I shall tell you a story
        about four little rabbits.
            whose names were—

Flopsy, Mopsy Cottontail

        and Peter

They lived with their mother in a
sand bank under the root of a
big fir tree.

'Now, my dears', said old Mrs Bunny
'you may go into the field or down
the lane, but don't go into Mr McGregor's
garden.'

Flopsy, Mopsy & Cottontail, who were good
little rabbits went down the lane to gather
blackberries, but Peter, who was very naughty

ran straight away to Mr McGregor's garden
and squeezed underneath the gate.
            First he ate some lettuce
        and some broad beans,
        then some radishes, and
        then feeling rather sick,
        he went to look for
        some parsley; but
        round the end of a
        cucumber frame
whom should he meet but Mr McGregor!

Mr McGregor was planting out young cabbages
but he jumped up & ran after Peter waving
a rake & calling out 'Stop thief'!

Peter was most dreadfully frightened &
rushed all over the garden, for he had
forgotten the way back to the gate.
He lost one of his shoes among the cabbages

*Above and right: Beatrix Potter's picture letter to Noel Moore,
sent from Scotland in 1893*

and the other shoe amongst the potatoes. After losing them he ran on four legs & went faster, so that I think he would

have got away altogether, if he had not unfortunately run into a gooseberry net and got caught fast by the large buttons on his jacket. It was a blue jacket with brass buttons; quite new.

Mr McGregor came up with a basket which he intended to pop on the top of Peter, but Peter wriggled out just in time, leaving his jacket behind,

and this time he found the gate, slipped underneath and ran home safely.

Mr McGregor hung up the little jacket & shoes for a scarecrow, to frighten the blackbirds.

Peter was ill during the evening, in consequence of over eating himself. His mother put him to bed and gave him a dose of camomile tea,

but Flopsy, Mopsy, and Cottontail had bread and milk and blackberries for supper.   I am coming back to London next Thursday, so I hope I shall see you soon, and the new baby. I remain, dear Noel, yours affectionately
                              Beatrix Potter.

Canon Hardwicke Rawnsley

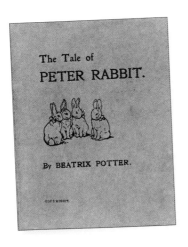

A first edition copy of The Tale of Peter Rabbit, *privately printed in 1901*

Canon Hardwicke Rawnsley, a friend of the Potter family and their local vicar in the Lake District, was the author of a popular collection of moral poems for children. With his help, the manuscript of *The Tale of Peter Rabbit* was sent to at least six publishers. Incredible though it now seems, one by one, these publishers rejected it! Undaunted, Beatrix had 250 copies of her story printed privately and those that she did not give away as presents she sold for 1/2d. Meanwhile, Beatrix and Canon Rawnsley continued to search for a commercial publisher for the book. Frederick Warne & Co. was interested in publishing the story, but strongly felt that colour illustrations were needed. Initially, Beatrix was against using colour, feeling it would be too expensive and also citing the 'rather uninteresting colour of a good many of the subjects which are most of them rabbit brown and green.' Once they persuaded Beatrix to use colour, Warne agreed to publish the story in 1902.

As in all her Tales, Beatrix used simple, direct language and never patronised her young readers. She tested out her prose on friends' children and responded to their requests. Much of the appeal of her Tales comes from their blend of light relief and serious undertones. Though most of the stories have happy endings, the characters do suffer the consequences of their actions: Peter, for instance, goes to bed with a stomach ache as a result of overindulgence in Mr. McGregor's garden. Many letters were exchanged between Beatrix and her publishers, her strong character emerging in the correspondence as the book progressed. Beatrix was interested in all aspects of book production. She had decided, informed opinions about everything from price and design, to format and the quality of the colour printing. Beatrix wanted the book to be as cheap as possible, so that children could afford to buy it with their pocket money. She was equally emphatic that the book be small, to accommodate little hands.

By the end of 1903 over 50,000 copies of *The Tale of Peter Rabbit* had been sold. 'The public must be fond of rabbits!' wrote Beatrix, 'What an appalling quantity of Peter.' *The Tale of Peter Rabbit* is as appealing today as when the story was first published, and

Beatrix's Peter Rabbit doll had lead shot inside its feet to make it stand upright.

Beatrix had a theory to explain its success. She wrote in 1905, 'It is much more satisfactory to address a real live child; I often think that that was the secret of the success of Peter Rabbit, it was written to a child—not made to order.' A keen businesswoman, Beatrix paid close attention to what her audience wanted and looked for ways to capitalise on her popular creations. Soon after *The Tale of Peter Rabbit* was published, she began to make a Peter Rabbit doll. 'I am cutting out calico patterns of Peter, I have not got it right yet, but the expression is going to be lovely; especially the whiskers—(pulled out of a brush!).' She registered her doll at the Patent office in London on 28th December 1903. The doll was followed the next year by wallpaper and then a Peter Rabbit board game devised by Beatrix herself.

There has been much speculation about the setting for the story, but Beatrix herself did not know for sure which Lakeland location had inspired her when she wrote the picture letter to Noel. In a letter written in 1942, she wrote, 'Peter was so composite and scattered in locality that I have found it troublesome to explain its various sources . . .' But although there is not one specific local setting for the story, the real Peter Rabbit, who was Beatrix's

A watercolour of Peter Rabbit, painted in 1899

Beatrix with Benjamin Bouncer on a lead in 1891

pet, is well known. Beatrix's rabbit, Peter Piper, lived to be eight years old and used to stretch out in front of the fire on the hearth rug like a cat. Beatrix never forgot the hero of her first little book. In one of her privately printed copies of *The Tale of Peter Rabbit* she wrote, 'In affectionate remembrance of poor old Peter Rabbit . . . whatever the limitations of his intellect or shortcomings of his fur, and his ears and toes, his disposition was uniformly amiable and his temper unfailingly sweet. An affectionate companion and a quiet friend.'

Beatrix Potter spent the summer of 1903 at Fawe Park, a large country house with a beautiful garden on the shore of Derwentwater. Soon after she arrived, she sent her editor, Norman Warne, a draft of what she called 'the rabbit story,' a sequel to *The Tale of Peter Rabbit*. Beatrix Potter modelled the hero of *The Tale of Benjamin Bunny* on her first pet rabbit, who had been smuggled into the nursery in a paper bag. His name was Benjamin H. Bouncer, or Bounce for short, and he was very fond of hot buttered toast and sweets. She described him as 'a noisy, cheerful determined animal, inclined to attack strangers'. *The Tale of Benjamin Bunny* continued the exploits of Peter Rabbit, who had wandered into Mr. McGregor's garden and very nearly ended up in a pie. Now, joined by his self-possessed cousin Benjamin, Peter sets out to recover his lost clothes from the scarecrow in the garden and has many adventures on the way.

A few weeks later, Beatrix Potter informed Norman Warne that she was making good progress with the drawings, and on 27th August she wrote, 'I have drawn a good many sketches for backgrounds of rabbits already which is perhaps as well, as the rain has come here at last.' By the end of the summer the backgrounds for *The Tale of Benjamin Bunny* were completed. Back in London Beatrix settled down for the winter months to continue working on the new book. In the middle of February 1904 Beatrix Potter wrote to Warne, 'I have nearly finished B. Bunny except the cat.'

Over the course of working together on five books, Beatrix and her editor had established a warm rapport. Though Beatrix's visits to the Frederick Warne offices were always chaperoned, the two exchanged letters nearly every day which allowed their friendship to flourish. On 25th July 1905, Norman Warne sent Beatrix a proposal of marriage, which she immediately accepted despite her parents' disapproval. At 39 years of age, Beatrix was determined to follow her heart, though she did appease her parents by keeping the engagement a secret. Unfortunately, only one month later, Norman died suddenly from a form of leukemia while Beatrix was on holiday with her family. Devastated, Beatrix took solace in her work. Earlier that summer Beatrix had used her book royalties to purchase Hill Top Farm, a working farm in the Lake District village of Near Sawrey. She drew inspiration from the tranquil surrounding landscape and set to work on her next books.

In the early months of 1909 Beatrix put the finishing touches to a new story about Peter Rabbit and Benjamin Bunny. 'I have done lots of sketches —not all to the purpose—and will now endeavour to finish up the F. Bunnies without further delay.'

Six pencil studies of Benjamin, drawn in 1890

Norman Warne

A preliminary watercolour drawing of the country gardens at Gwaynynog

The Tale of The Flopsy Bunnies is set in the garden of her uncle's house, Gwaynynog, in Wales, a charming old house in the middle of a rambling country garden which Beatrix loved to sketch. Always at her best when painting rabbits, flowers and gardens, Beatrix used her skills to great advantage when illustrating this little book. A number of her preliminary sketches for the garden scenes have survived and they show the care she took to prepare each illustration.

It was natural for Beatrix to invite her readers to find out what had happened to the grown-up Peter Rabbit and his naughty cousin. The villain of the tale is Mr. McGregor again, but Benjamin Bunny is now married to Peter Rabbit's sister, Flopsy, and the six Flopsy Bunnies of the title are their children. Beatrix recognised that her readers enjoyed the 'independence' of her characters. She understood that they liked to imagine Benjamin and Peter 'busily absorbed in their own doings'— even marrying and having a family—long after the story was over and the book was closed. Fond of the Flopsy Bunnies, Beatrix wrote about their adventures again as part of her collection of miniature letters for the children she knew. She wrote some tiny letters which appear to come from various little Flopsy bunnies. The letters decrease

Miniature letters from the Flopsy Bunnies, sent by Beatrix to a young reader

in size and content according to the age and size of each little brother and sister rabbit, until those supposedly written by the tiniest bunnies are nothing more than a scribble and a few kisses.

Benjamin and Flopsy's large family, which they have great difficulty keeping track of, was the subject for another little book published in 1912. *The Tale of Mr. Tod* is about the kidnapping of the bunnies by an unpleasant badger named Tommy Brock. Tommy Brock brings the baby rabbits to the house of Mr. Tod, the fox, and very nearly eats them. Disaster is only averted when a terrific battle between Mr. Tod and his uninvited house guest distracts the two predators from the bunnies. Once again, Benjamin turns to his cousin Peter for assistance, and together they stage a daring rescue of the babies. Another of Peter's sisters, Cottontail, makes a brief appearance when she points the rescue party in the right direction.

A long, rather dark Tale featuring disagreeable principal characters, *The Tale of Mr. Tod* marked a change from writing what Beatrix described as, 'goody goody books about nice people'. Due to her preoccupation with her new farming career, Beatrix had less time for painting and therefore the majority of the book's illustrations are framed line drawings in the style of woodcuts. The watercolours included, however, feature real-life landscapes of Sawrey. Bull Banks, where Mr. Tod lives in summer, was a pasture on Castle Farm, where Beatrix now lived. Mr. Tod is also depicted walking along the banks of Esthwaite Water, one of Beatrix's favourite Lakeland views.

Although Beatrix's publishers worried that the protagonists in *The Tale of Mr. Tod* were unlikeable, Beatrix knew that children enjoyed reading about misconduct. *The Story of A Fierce Bad Rabbit*, published in 1906, was written for her

Beatrix's watercolour painting of the banks of Esthwaite Water

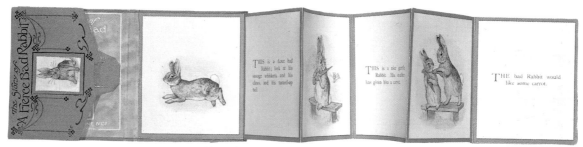

A first edition copy of The Story of A Fierce Bad Rabbit, *in panorama format*

editor's daughter. This little girl had complained that Peter was too good a rabbit and that she wanted a story about a *really* naughty one. Intended for very young children, this simple story was first published as a panorama, unfolding in a long strip of pictures and text from a wallet with a tuck-in flap. This format proved unpopular with booksellers, as the picture strips tended to get unrolled, and the story was reprinted in book form in 1916.

A year after the publication of *The Tale of Mr. Tod*, Beatrix married William Heelis at the age of 47. Settling permanently in the Lake District with her solicitor husband, Beatrix became increasingly engrossed in her second career as a farmer and lost interest in her writing and illustrating. Her eyes were beginning to weaken and, as she complained good-naturedly to her editor at Frederick Warne in 1918, 'Somehow when one is up to the eyes in work with real live animals it makes one despise paper-book-animals—but I mustn't say that to my publisher!' Interested in preserving traditional farming methods, Beatrix began to breed Herdwick sheep, a variety native to the Lake District. She also bought large stretches of beautiful Lakeland countryside with her book royalties. A pioneering member of the National Trust, Beatrix recognised the importance of conserving the countryside from the destruction of industry and holidaymakers. When she died in 1943, Beatrix left her land and 15 farms to the nation for future generations to enjoy.

Today, *The Tale of Peter Rabbit* has been translated into 28 languages and is published all

Beatrix and William Heelis on their wedding day, 15th October 1913

Peter Rabbit's Race Game, based on a 1907 design by Beatrix, was published in 1917.

over the world. Timeless classics, the books continue to sell in their millions and have been treasured by generations of children. Today Peter can be found on products ranging from baby clothes to chocolates. This merchandising began with Beatrix Potter's own interest in finding new ways to explore and expand the imaginary world she had created. Enjoying business negotiations, Beatrix was actively involved in developing what she called her 'sideshows'. Beatrix always took care to ensure that the reproduction of her characters on merchandise—whether on china tea sets, wooden figurines, dolls or painting books—was faithful to the original and retained the magic of the very first little 'rabbit book'. Towards the end of her life Beatrix Potter wrote, 'If I have done anything—even a little—to help small children on the road to enjoy and appreciate honest, simple pleasures, I have done a bit of good.' She was a remarkable woman, with a truly original imagination, artistic and literary talent, vision and the strength of mind to find creative fulfilment.

Above and below: Early Peter Rabbit merchandise

THE TALE OF
PETER RABBIT

1902

ONCE upon a time there were four little Rabbits, and their names were—

Flopsy,
Mopsy,
Cotton-tail,
and Peter.

They lived with their Mother in a sand-bank, underneath the root of a very big fir-tree.

"Now, my dears," said old Mrs. Rabbit one morning, "you may go into the fields or down the lane, but don't go into Mr. McGregor's garden: your Father had an accident there; he was put in a pie by Mrs. McGregor.

"Now run along, and don't get into mischief. I am going out."

Then old Mrs. Rabbit took a basket and her umbrella, and went through the wood to the baker's. She bought a loaf of brown bread and five currant buns.

Flopsy, Mopsy, and Cotton-tail, who were good little bunnies, went down the lane to gather blackberries.

But Peter, who was very naughty, ran straight away to Mr. McGregor's garden, and squeezed under the gate!

First he ate some lettuces and some French beans; and then he ate some radishes.

And then, feeling rather sick, he went to look for some parsley.

But round the end of a cucumber frame, whom should he meet but Mr. McGregor!

Mr. McGregor was on his hands and knees planting out young cabbages, but he jumped up and ran after Peter, waving a rake and calling out, "Stop thief!"

Peter was most dreadfully frightened; he rushed all over the garden, for he had forgotten the way back to the gate.

He lost one of his shoes among the cabbages, and the other shoe amongst the potatoes.

After losing them, he ran on four legs and went faster, so that I think he might have got away altogether if he had not unfortunately run into a gooseberry net, and got caught by the large buttons on his jacket.

It was a blue jacket with brass buttons, quite new.

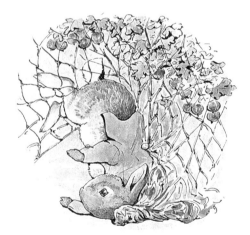

Peter gave himself up for lost, and shed big tears; but his sobs were overheard by some friendly sparrows, who flew to him in great excitement, and implored him to exert himself.

Mr. McGregor came up with a sieve, which he intended to pop upon the top of Peter; but Peter wriggled out just in time, leaving his jacket behind him.

And rushed into the tool-shed, and jumped into a can. It would have been a beautiful thing to hide in, if it had not had so much water in it.

Mr. McGregor was quite sure that Peter was somewhere in the tool-shed, perhaps hidden underneath a flower-pot. He began to turn them over carefully, looking under each.

Presently Peter sneezed—"Kertyschoo!" Mr. McGregor was after him in no time.

And tried to put his foot upon Peter, who jumped out of a window, upsetting three plants. The window was too small for Mr. McGregor, and he was tired of running after Peter. He went back to his work.

Peter sat down to rest; he was out of breath and trembling with fright, and he had not the least idea which way to go.

Also he was very damp with sitting in that can.

After a time he began to wander about, going lippity—lippity—not very fast, and looking all round.

He found a door in a wall; but it was locked, and there was no room for a fat little rabbit to squeeze underneath.

An old mouse was running in and out over the stone door-step, carrying peas and beans to her family in the wood. Peter asked her the way to the gate, but she had such a large pea in her mouth that she could not answer. She only shook her head at him. Peter began to cry.

Then he tried to find his way straight across the garden, but he became more and more puzzled. Presently, he came to a pond where Mr. McGregor filled his water-cans. A white cat was staring at some gold-fish, she sat very, very still, but now and then the tip of her tail twitched as if it were alive. Peter thought it best to go away without speaking to her; he had heard about cats from his cousin, little Benjamin Bunny.

He went back towards the tool-shed, but suddenly, quite close to him, he heard the noise of a hoe —scr-r-ritch, scratch, scratch, scritch. Peter scuttered underneath the bushes. But presently, as nothing happened, he came out, and climbed upon a wheelbarrow and peeped over. The first thing he saw was Mr. McGregor hoeing onions. His back was turned towards Peter, and beyond him was the gate!

Peter got down very quietly off the wheelbarrow, and started running as fast as he could go, along a straight walk behind some black-currant bushes.

Mr. McGregor caught sight of him at the corner, but Peter did not care. He slipped underneath the gate, and was safe at last in the wood outside the garden.

Mr. McGregor hung up the little jacket and the shoes for a scarecrow to frighten the blackbirds.

Peter never stopped running or looked behind him till he got home to the big fir-tree.

He was so tired that he flopped down upon the nice soft sand on the floor of the rabbit-hole and shut his eyes. His mother was busy cooking; she wondered what he had done with his clothes. It was the second little jacket and pair of shoes that Peter had lost in a fortnight!

I am sorry to say that Peter was not very well during the evening.

His mother put him to bed, and made some camomile tea; and she gave a dose of it to Peter!

"One table-spoonful to be taken at bed-time."

But Flopsy, Mopsy, and Cottontail had bread and milk and blackberries for supper.

THE END

THE TALE OF
BENJAMIN BUNNY

1904

ONE morning a little
rabbit sat on a bank.
He pricked his ears and
listened to the trit-trot,
trit-trot of a pony.

A gig was coming along
the road; it was driven by
Mr. McGregor, and beside
him sat Mrs. McGregor in
her best bonnet.

As soon as they had
passed, little Benjamin
Bunny slid down into the
road, and set off—with a
hop, skip and a jump—to
call upon his relations, who
lived in the wood at the
back of Mr. McGregor's
garden.

That wood was full of rabbit holes; and in the neatest sandiest hole of all, lived Benjamin's aunt and his cousins—Flopsy, Mopsy, Cotton-tail and Peter.

Old Mrs. Rabbit was a widow; she earned her living by knitting rabbit-wool mittens and muffetees (I once bought a pair at a bazaar). She also sold herbs, and rosemary tea, and rabbit-tobacco (which is what *we* call lavender).

Little Benjamin did not very much want to see his Aunt.

He came round the back of the fir-tree, and nearly tumbled upon the top of his Cousin Peter.

Peter was sitting by himself. He looked poorly, and was dressed in a red cotton pocket-handkerchief.

"Peter,"—said little Benjamin, in a whisper—"who has got your clothes?"

Peter replied—"The scarecrow in Mr. McGregor's garden," and described how he had been chased about the garden, and had dropped his shoes and coat.

Little Benjamin sat down beside his cousin, and assured him that Mr. McGregor had gone out in a gig, and Mrs. McGregor also; and certainly for the day, because she was wearing her best bonnet.

Peter said he hoped that it would rain.

At this point, old Mrs. Rabbit's voice was heard inside the rabbit hole, calling—"Cotton-tail! Cotton-tail! Fetch some more camomile!"

Peter said he thought he might feel better if he went for a walk.

They went away hand in hand, and got upon the flat top of the wall at the bottom of the wood. From here they looked down into Mr. McGregor's garden. Peter's coat and shoes were plainly to be seen upon the scare-crow, topped with an old tam-o-shanter of Mr. McGregor's.

Little Benjamin said, "It spoils people's clothes to squeeze under a gate; the proper way to get in, is to climb down a pear tree."

Peter fell down head first; but it was of no consequence, as the bed below was newly raked and quite soft.

It had been sown with lettuces.

They left a great many odd little foot-marks all over the bed, especially little Benjamin, who was wearing clogs.

Little Benjamin said that the first thing to be done was to get back Peter's clothes, in order that they might be able to use the pocket-handkerchief.

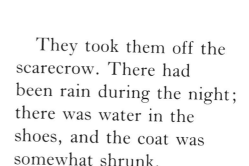

They took them off the scarecrow. There had been rain during the night; there was water in the shoes, and the coat was somewhat shrunk.

Benjamin tried on the tam-o-shanter, but it was too big for him.

Then he suggested that they should fill the pocket-handkerchief with onions, as a little present for his Aunt.

Peter did not seem to be enjoying himself; he kept hearing noises.

Benjamin, on the contrary, was perfectly at home, and ate a lettuce leaf. He said that he was in the habit of coming to the garden with his father to get lettuces for their Sunday dinner.

(The name of little Benjamin's papa was old Mr. Benjamin Bunny.)

The lettuces certainly were very fine.

Peter did not eat anything; he said he should like to go home. Presently he dropped half the onions.

Little Benjamin said that it was not possible to get back up the pear-tree, with a load of vegetables. He led the way boldly towards the other end of the garden. They went along a little walk on planks, under a sunny red-brick wall.

The mice sat on their door-steps cracking cherry-stones, they winked at Peter Rabbit and little Benjamin Bunny.

Presently Peter let the pocket-handkerchief go again.

They got amongst flowerpots, and frames and tubs; Peter heard noises worse than ever, his eyes were as big as lolly-pops!

He was a step or two in front of his cousin, when he suddenly stopped.

This is what those little rabbits saw round that corner!

Little Benjamin took one look, and then, in half a minute less than no time, he hid himself and Peter and the onions underneath a large basket . . .

The cat got up and stretched herself, and came and sniffed at the basket.

Perhaps she liked the smell of onions!

Anyway, she sat down upon the top of the basket.

She sat there for *five hours*.

*   *   *

I cannot draw you a picture of Peter and Benjamin underneath the basket, because it was quite dark, and because the smell of onions was fearful; it made Peter Rabbit and little Benjamin cry.

The sun got round behind the wood, and it was quite late in the afternoon; but still the cat sat upon the basket.

At length there was a pitter-patter, pitter-patter, and some bits of mortar fell from the wall above.

The cat looked up and saw old Mr. Benjamin Bunny prancing along the top of the wall of the upper terrace.

He was smoking a pipe of rabbit-tobacco, and had a little switch in his hand.

He was looking for his son.

Old Mr. Bunny had no opinion whatever of cats.

He took a tremendous jump off the top of the wall on to the top of the cat, and cuffed it off the basket, and kicked it into the green-house, scratching off a handful of fur.

The cat was too much surprised to scratch back.

When old Mr. Bunny had driven the cat into the green-house, he locked the door.

Then he came back to the basket and took out his son Benjamin by the ears, and whipped him with the little switch.

Then he took out his nephew Peter.

Then he took out the handkerchief of onions, and marched out of the garden.

When Mr. McGregor returned about half an hour later, he observed several things which perplexed him.

It looked as though some person had been walking all over the garden in a pair of clogs—only the foot-marks were too ridiculously little!

Also he could not under-stand how the cat could have managed to shut herself up *inside* the green-house, locking the door upon the *outside*.

When Peter got home, his mother forgave him, because she was so glad to see that he had found his shoes and coat. Cotton-tail and Peter folded up the pocket-handkerchief, and old Mrs. Rabbit strung up the onions and hung them from the kitchen ceiling, with the bunches of herbs and the rabbit-tobacco.

THE END

THE TALE OF
THE
FLOPSY BUNNIES

1909

IT is said that the effect of eating too much lettuce is "soporific".

I have never felt sleepy after eating lettuces; but then *I* am not a rabbit.

They certainly had a very soporific effect upon the Flopsy Bunnies!

When Benjamin Bunny grew up, he married his Cousin Flopsy. They had a large family, and they were very improvident and cheerful.

I do not remember the separate names of their children; they were generally called the "Flopsy Bunnies".

As there was not always quite enough to eat—Benjamin used to borrow cabbages from Flopsy's brother, Peter Rabbit, who kept a nursery garden.

Sometimes Peter Rabbit had no cabbages to spare.

When this happened, the Flopsy Bunnies went across the field to a rubbish heap, in the ditch outside Mr. McGregor's garden.

Mr. McGregor's rubbish heap was a mixture. There were jam pots and paper bags, and mountains of chopped grass from the mowing machine (which always tasted oily), and some rotten vegetable marrows and an old boot or two. One day—oh joy!—there were a quantity of overgrown lettuces, which had "shot" into flower.

The Flopsy Bunnies simply stuffed
lettuces. By degrees, one after
another, they were overcome with
slumber, and lay down in the
mown grass.

Benjamin was not so much
overcome as his children. Before
going to sleep he was sufficiently
wide awake to put a paper bag
over his head to keep off the flies.

The little Flopsy Bunnies
slept delightfully in the warm
sun. From the lawn beyond
the garden came the distant
clacketty sound of the mowing
machine. The blue-bottles
buzzed about the wall, and a
little old mouse picked over
the rubbish among the jam
pots.

(I can tell you her name, she was
called Thomasina Tittlemouse, a
woodmouse with a long tail.)

She rustled across the paper bag,
and awakened Benjamin Bunny.

The mouse apologized profusely,
and said that she knew Peter Rabbit.

While she and Benjamin were talking, close under the wall, they heard a heavy tread above their heads; and suddenly Mr. McGregor emptied out a sackful of lawn mowings right upon the top of the sleeping Flopsy Bunnies! Benjamin shrank down under his paper bag. The mouse hid in a jam pot.

The little rabbits smiled sweetly in their sleep under the shower of grass; they did not awake because the lettuces had been so soporific.

They dreamt that their mother Flopsy was tucking them up in a hay bed.

Mr. McGregor looked down after emptying his sack. He saw some funny little brown tips of ears sticking up through the lawn mowings. He stared at them for some time.

Presently a fly settled on one of them and it moved.

Mr. McGregor climbed down on to the rubbish heap—

"One, two, three, four! five! six leetle rabbits!" said he as he dropped them into his sack.

The Flopsy Bunnies dreamt that their mother was turning them over in bed. They stirred a little in their sleep, but still they did not wake up.

Mr. McGregor tied up the sack and left it on the wall.

He went to put away the mowing machine.

While he was gone, Mrs. Flopsy Bunny (who had remained at home) came across the field.

She looked suspiciously at the sack and wondered where everybody was?

Then the mouse came out of her jam pot, and Benjamin took the paper bag off his head, and they told the doleful tale.

Benjamin and Flopsy were in despair, they could not undo the string.

But Mrs. Tittlemouse was a resourceful person. She nibbled a hole in the bottom corner of the sack.

The little rabbits were pulled out and pinched to wake them.

Their parents stuffed the empty sack with three rotten vegetable marrows, an old blacking-brush and two decayed turnips.

Then they all hid under a bush and watched for Mr. McGregor.

Mr. McGregor came back and picked up the sack, and carried it off.

He carried it hanging down, as if it were rather heavy.

The Flopsy Bunnies followed at a safe distance.

They watched him go into his house.

And then they crept up to the window to listen.

Mr. McGregor threw down the sack on the stone floor in a way that would have been extremely painful to the Flopsy Bunnies, if they had happened to have been inside it.

They could hear him drag his chair on the flags, and chuckle—

"One, two, three, four, five, six leetle rabbits!" said Mr. McGregor.

"Eh? What's that? What have they been spoiling now?" inquired Mrs. McGregor.

"One, two, three, four, five, six leetle fat rabbits!" repeated Mr. McGregor, counting on his fingers—"one, two, three—"

"Don't you be silly; what do you mean, you silly old man?"

"In the sack! One, two, three, four, five, six!" replied Mr. McGregor.

(The youngest Flopsy Bunny got upon the window-sill.)

Mrs. McGregor took hold of the sack and felt it. She said she could feel six, but they must be *old* rabbits, because they were so hard and all different shapes.

"Not fit to eat; but the skins will do fine to line my old cloak."

"Line your old cloak?" shouted Mr. McGregor—"I shall sell them and buy myself baccy!"

"Rabbit tobacco! I shall skin them and cut off their heads."

Mrs. McGregor untied the sack and put her hand inside.

When she felt the vegetables she became very very angry. She said that Mr. McGregor had "done it a purpose".

And Mr. McGregor was very angry too. One of the rotten marrows came flying through the kitchen window, and hit the youngest Flopsy Bunny.

It was rather hurt.

Then Benjamin and Flopsy thought that it was time to go home.

So Mr. McGregor did not get his tobacco, and Mrs. McGregor did not get her rabbit skins.

But next Christmas Thomasina Tittlemouse got a present of enough rabbit-wool to make herself a cloak and a hood, and a handsome muff and a pair of warm mittens.

THE END

THE TALE OF
MR. TOD

1912

I have made many books about well-behaved people. Now, for a change, I am going to make a story about two disagreeable people, called Tommy Brock and Mr. Tod.

Nobody could call Mr. Tod "nice". The rabbits could not bear him; they could smell him half a mile off. He was of a wandering habit and he had foxey whiskers; they never knew where he would be next.

One day he was living in a stick-house in the coppice, causing terror to the family of old Mr. Benjamin Bouncer. Next day he moved into a pollard willow near the lake, frightening the wild ducks and the water rats.

In winter and early spring he might generally be found in an earth amongst the rocks at the top of Bull Banks, under Oatmeal Crag.

He had half a dozen houses, but he was seldom at home.

The houses were not always empty when Mr. Tod moved *out*; because sometimes Tommy Brock moved *in;* (without asking leave).

Tommy Brock was a short bristly fat waddling person with a grin; he grinned all over his face. He was not nice in his habits.

He ate wasp nests and frogs and worms; and he waddled about by moonlight, digging things up.

His clothes were very dirty; and as he slept in the day-time, he always went to bed in his boots. And the bed which he went to bed in, was generally Mr. Tod's.

Now Tommy Brock did occasionally eat rabbit-pie; but it was only very little young ones occasionally, when other food was really scarce. He was friendly with old Mr. Bouncer; they agreed in disliking the wicked otters and Mr. Tod; they often talked over that painful subject.

Old Mr. Bouncer was stricken in years. He sat in the spring sunshine outside the burrow, in a muffler; smoking a pipe of rabbit tobacco.

He lived with his son Benjamin Bunny and his daughter-in-law Flopsy, who had a young family. Old Mr. Bouncer was in charge of the family that afternoon, because Benjamin and Flopsy had gone out.

The little rabbit-babies were just old enough to open their blue eyes and kick. They lay in a fluffy bed of rabbit wool and hay, in a shallow burrow, separate from the main rabbit hole. To tell the truth—old Mr. Bouncer had forgotten them.

He sat in the sun, and conversed cordially with Tommy Brock, who was passing through the wood with a sack and a little spud which he used for digging, and some mole traps. He complained bitterly about the scarcity of pheasants' eggs, and accused Mr. Tod of poaching them. And the otters had cleared

off all the frogs while he was asleep in winter—"I have not had a good square meal for a fortnight, I am living on pig-nuts. I shall have to turn vegetarian and eat my own tail!" said Tommy Brock.

It was not much of a joke, but it tickled old Mr. Bouncer; because Tommy Brock was so fat and stumpy and grinning.

So old Mr. Bouncer laughed; and pressed Tommy Brock to come inside, to taste a slice of seed-cake and "a glass of my daughter Flopsy's cowslip wine". Tommy Brock squeezed himself into the rabbit hole with alacrity.

Then old Mr. Bouncer smoked another pipe, and gave Tommy Brock a cabbage leaf cigar which was so very strong that it made Tommy Brock grin more than ever; and the smoke filled the burrow. Old Mr. Bouncer coughed and laughed; and Tommy Brock puffed and grinned.

And Mr. Bouncer laughed and coughed, and shut his eyes because of the cabbage smoke . . .

When Flopsy and Benjamin came back—old Mr. Bouncer woke up. Tommy Brock and all the young rabbit-babies had disappeared!

Mr. Bouncer would not confess that he had admitted anybody into the rabbit hole. But the smell of badger was undeniable; and there were round heavy footmarks in the sand. He was in disgrace; Flopsy wrung her ears, and slapped him.

Benjamin Bunny set off at once after Tommy Brock.

There was not much difficulty in tracking him; he had left his footmark and gone slowly up the winding footpath through the wood. Here he had rooted up the moss and wood sorrel. There he had dug quite a deep hole for dog darnel; and had set a mole trap. A little stream crossed the way. Benjamin skipped lightly over dry-foot; the badger's heavy steps showed plainly in the mud.

The path led to a part of the thicket where the trees had been cleared; there were leafy oak stumps, and a sea of blue hyacinths—but the smell that made Benjamin stop, was *not* the smell of flowers!

Mr. Tod's stick house was before him and, for once, Mr. Tod was at home. There was not only a foxey flavour in proof of it—there was smoke coming out of the broken pail that served as a chimney.

Benjamin Bunny sat up, staring; his whiskers twitched. Inside the stick house somebody dropped a plate, and said something. Benjamin stamped his foot, and bolted.

He never stopped till he came to the other side of the wood. Apparently Tommy Brock had turned the same way. Upon the top of the wall, there were again the marks of badger; and some ravellings of a sack had caught on a briar.

Benjamin climbed over the wall, into a meadow. He found another mole trap newly set; he was still upon the track of Tommy Brock. It was getting late in the afternoon. Other rabbits were coming out to enjoy the evening air. One of them in a blue coat by himself, was busily hunting for dandelions.— "Cousin Peter! Peter Rabbit, Peter Rabbit!" shouted Benjamin Bunny.

The blue-coated rabbit sat up with pricked ears—

"Whatever is the matter, Cousin Benjamin? Is it a cat? or John Stoat Ferret?"

"No, no, no! He's bagged my family—Tommy Brock—in a sack—have you seen him?"

"Tommy Brock? How many, Cousin Benjamin?"

"Seven, Cousin Peter, and all of them twins! Did he come this way? Please tell me quick!"

"Yes, yes; not ten minutes since . . . he said they were *caterpillars;* I did think they were kicking rather hard, for caterpillars."

"Which way? Which way has he gone, Cousin Peter?"

"He had a sack with something 'live in it; I watched him set a mole trap. Let me use my mind, Cousin Benjamin; tell me from the beginning." Benjamin did so.

"My Uncle Bouncer has displayed a lamentable want of discretion for his years;" said Peter reflectively, "but there are two hopeful circumstances. Your family is alive and kicking; and Tommy Brock has had refreshment. He will probably go to sleep, and keep them for breakfast."

"Which way?"

"Cousin Benjamin, compose yourself. I know very well which way. Because Mr. Tod was at home in the stickhouse he has gone to Mr. Tod's other house, at the top of Bull Banks. I partly know, because he offered to leave any message at Sister Cottontail's; he said he would be passing." (Cottontail had married a black rabbit, and gone to live on the hill.)

Peter hid his dandelions, and accompanied the afflicted parent, who was all of a twitter. They crossed several fields and began to climb the hill; the tracks of Tommy Brock were plainly to be seen. He seemed to have put down the sack every dozen yards, to rest.

"He must be very puffed; we are close behind him, by the scent. What a nasty person!" said Peter.

The sunshine was still warm and slanting on the hill pastures. Half way up, Cottontail was sitting in her doorway, with four or five half-grown little rabbits playing about her; one black and the others brown.

Cottontail had seen Tommy Brock passing in the distance. Asked whether her husband was at home she replied that Tommy Brock had rested twice while she watched him.

He had nodded, and pointed to the sack, and seemed doubled up with laughing.—"Come away, Peter; he will be cooking them; come quicker!" said Benjamin Bunny.

They climbed up and up;—"He was at home; I saw his black ears peeping out of the hole." "They live too near the rocks to quarrel with their neighbours. Come on, Cousin Benjamin!"

When they came near the wood at the top of Bull Banks, they went cautiously. The trees grew amongst heaped-up rocks; and there, beneath a crag—Mr. Tod had made one of his homes. It was at the top of a steep bank; the rocks and bushes overhung it. The rabbits crept up carefully, listening and peeping.

This house was something between a cave, a prison, and a tumble-down pig-stye. There was a strong door, which was shut and locked.

The setting sun made the window panes glow like red flame; but the kitchen fire was not alight. It was neatly laid with dry sticks, as the rabbits could see, when they peeped through the window.

Benjamin sighed with relief.

But there were preparations upon the kitchen table which made him shudder. There was an immense empty pie-dish of

blue willow pattern, and a large carving knife and fork, and a chopper.

At the other end of the table was a partly unfolded tablecloth, a plate,

a tumbler,
a knife
and fork,
salt-cellar,
mustard
and a chair
—in short, preparations for one person's supper.

No person was to be seen, and no young rabbits. The kitchen was empty and silent; the clock had run down. Peter and Benjamin flattened their noses against the window, and stared into the dusk.

Then they scrambled round the rocks to the other side of the house. It was damp and smelly, and overgrown with thorns and briars.

The rabbits shivered in their shoes.

"Oh my poor rabbit babies! What a dreadful place; I shall never see them again!" sighed Benjamin.

They crept up to the bedroom window. It was closed and bolted like the kitchen. But there were signs that this window had been recently open; the cobwebs were disturbed, and there were fresh dirty footmarks upon the window-sill.

The room inside was so dark, that at first they could make out nothing; but they could hear a noise—a slow deep regular snoring grunt. And as their eyes became accustomed to the darkness, they perceived that somebody was asleep on Mr. Tod's bed, curled up under the blanket.—"He has gone to bed in his boots," whispered Peter.

Benjamin, who was all of a twitter, pulled Peter off the window-sill.

Tommy Brock's snores continued, grunty and regular from Mr. Tod's bed. Nothing could be seen of the young family.

The sun had set; an owl began to hoot in the wood. There were many unpleasant things lying about, that had much better have been buried; rabbit bones and skulls, and chickens' legs and other horrors. It was a shocking place, and very dark.

They went back to the front of the house, and tried in every way to move the bolt of the kitchen window. They tried to push up a rusty nail between the window sashes; but it was of no use, especially without a light.

They sat side by side outside the window, whispering and listening.

In half an hour the moon rose over the wood. It shone full and clear and cold, upon the house amongst the rocks, and in at the kitchen window. But alas, no little rabbit babies were to be seen!

The moonbeams twinkled on the carving knife and the pie-dish, and made a path of brightness across the dirty floor.

The light showed a little door in a wall beside the kitchen fireplace—a little iron door belonging to a brick oven, of that old-fashioned sort that used to be heated with faggots of wood.

And presently at the same moment Peter and Benjamin noticed that whenever they shook the window—the little door opposite shook in answer. The young family were alive; shut up in the oven!

Benjamin was so excited that it was a mercy he did not awake Tommy Brock, whose snores continued solemnly in Mr. Tod's bed.

But there really was not very much comfort in the discovery. They could not open the window; and although the young family was alive—the little rabbits were quite incapable of letting themselves out; they were not old enough to crawl.

After much whispering, Peter and Benjamin decided to dig a tunnel. They began to burrow a yard or two lower down the bank. They hoped that they might be able to work between the large stones under the house; the kitchen floor was so dirty that it was impossible to say whether it was made of earth or flags.

They dug and dug for hours. They could not tunnel straight on account of stones; but by the end of the night they were under the kitchen floor. Benjamin was on his back, scratching upwards. Peter's claws were worn down; he was outside the tunnel, shuffling sand away. He called out that it was morning— sunrise; and that the jays were making a noise down below in the woods.

Benjamin Bunny came out of the dark tunnel, shaking the sand from his ears; he cleaned his face with his paws. Every minute the sun shone warmer on the top of the hill. In the valley there was a sea of white mist, with golden tops of trees showing through.

Again from the fields down below in the mist there came the angry cry of a jay—followed by the sharp yelping bark of a fox!

Then those two rabbits lost their heads completely. They did the most foolish thing that they could have done. They rushed into their short new tunnel, and hid themselves at the top end of it, under Mr. Tod's kitchen floor.

Mr. Tod was coming up Bull Banks, and he was in the very worst of tempers. First he had been upset by breaking the plate. It was his own fault; but it was a china plate, the last of the dinner service that had belonged to his grandmother, old Vixen Tod. Then the midges had been very bad. And he had

failed to catch a hen pheasant on her nest; and it had contained only five eggs, two of them addled. Mr. Tod had had an unsatisfactory night.

As usual, when out of humour, he determined to move house. First he tried the pollard willow, but it was damp; and the otters had left a dead fish near it. Mr. Tod likes nobody's leavings but his own.

He made his way up the hill; his temper was not improved by noticing unmistakable marks of badger. No one else grubs up the moss so wantonly as Tommy Brock.

Mr. Tod slapped his stick upon the earth and fumed; he guessed

where Tommy Brock had gone to. He was further annoyed by the jay bird which followed him persistently. It flew from tree to tree and scolded, warning every rabbit within hearing that either a cat or a fox was coming up the plantation. Once when it flew screaming over his head—Mr. Tod snapped at it, and barked.

He approached his house very carefully, with a large rusty key. He sniffed and his whiskers bristled. The house was locked up, but Mr. Tod had his doubts whether it was empty. He turned the rusty key in the lock; the rabbits below could hear it. Mr. Tod opened the door cautiously and went in.

The sight that met Mr. Tod's eyes in Mr. Tod's kitchen made Mr. Tod furious. There was Mr. Tod's chair, and Mr. Tod's pie-dish, and his knife and fork and mustard and salt-cellar and his tablecloth that he had left folded up in the dresser—all set out for supper (or breakfast)—without doubt for that odious Tommy Brock.

There was a smell of fresh earth and dirty badger, which fortunately overpowered all smell of rabbit

But what absorbed Mr. Tod's attention was a noise—a deep slow regular snoring grunting noise, coming from his own bed.

He peeped through the hinges of the half-open bedroom door. Then he turned and came out of the house

in a hurry. His whiskers bristled and his coat-collar stood on end with rage.

For the next twenty minutes Mr. Tod kept creeping cautiously into the house, and retreating hurriedly out again. By degrees he ventured further in—right into the bedroom. When he was outside the house, he scratched up the earth with fury. But when he was inside—he did not like the look of Tommy Brock's teeth.

He was lying on his back with his mouth open, grinning from ear to ear. He snored peacefully and regularly; but one eye was not perfectly shut.

Mr Tod came in and out of the bedroom. Twice he brought in his walking-stick, and once he brought in the coal-scuttle. But he thought better of it, and took them away.

When he came back after removing the coal-scuttle, Tommy Brock was lying a little more sideways; but he seemed even sounder asleep. He was an incurably indolent person; he was not in the least afraid of Mr. Tod; he was simply too lazy and comfortable to move.

Mr. Tod came back yet again into the bedroom with a clothes line. He stood a minute watching Tommy Brock and listening attentively to the snores. They were very loud indeed, but seemed quite natural.

Mr. Tod turned his back towards the bed, and undid the window. It creaked; he turned round with a jump. Tommy Brock, who had opened one eye—shut it hastily. The snores continued.

Mr. Tod's proceedings were peculiar, and rather uneasy (because the bed was between the window and the door of the bedroom). He opened the

window a little way, and pushed out the greater part of the clothes line on to the window-sill. The rest of the line, with a hook at the end, remained in his hand.

Tommy Brock snored conscientiously. Mr. Tod stood and looked at him for a minute; then he left the room again.

Tommy Brock opened both eyes, and looked at the rope and grinned. There was a noise outside the window. Tommy Brock shut his eyes in a hurry.

Mr. Tod had gone out at the front door, and round to the back of the house. On the way, he stumbled over the rabbit burrow. If he had had any idea who was inside it, he would have pulled them out quickly.

His foot went through the tunnel nearly upon the top of Peter Rabbit and Benjamin, but fortunately he thought that it was some more of Tommy Brock's work.

He took up the coil of line from the sill, listened for a moment, and then tied the rope to a tree.

Tommy Brock watched him with one eye, through the window. He was puzzled.

Mr. Tod fetched a large heavy pailful of water from the spring, and staggered with it through the kitchen into his bedroom.

Tommy Brock snored industriously, with rather a snort.

Mr. Tod put down the pail beside the bed, took up the end of rope with the hook—hesitated, and looked at Tommy Brock. The snores were almost apoplectic; but the grin was not quite so big.

Mr. Tod gingerly mounted a chair by the head of the bedstead. His legs were dangerously near to Tommy Brock's teeth.

He reached up and put the end of rope, with the hook, over the head of the tester bed, where the curtains ought to hang.

(Mr. Tod's curtains were folded up, and put away, owing to the house being unoccupied. So was the counterpane. Tommy Brock was covered with a blanket only.) Mr. Tod standing on the unsteady chair looked down upon him attentively; he really was a first prize sound sleeper!

It seemed as though nothing would waken him—not even the flapping rope across the bed.

Mr. Tod descended safely from the chair, and endeavoured to get up again with the pail of water. He intended to hang it from the hook, dangling over the head of Tommy Brock, in order to make a sort of shower-bath, worked by a string, through the window.

But naturally being a thin-legged person (though vindictive and sandy whiskered)—he was quite unable to lift the heavy weight to the level of the hook and rope. He very nearly over-balanced himself.

The snores became more and more apoplectic. One of Tommy Brock's hind legs twitched under the blanket, but still he slept on peacefully.

Mr. Tod and the pail descended from the chair without accident. After considerable thought, he emptied the water into a wash-basin and jug. The empty pail was not too heavy for him; he slung it up wobbling over the head of Tommy Brock.

Surely there never was such a sleeper! Mr. Tod got up and down, down and up on the chair.

As he could not lift the whole pailful of water at once, he fetched a milk jug, and ladled quarts of water into the pail by degrees. The pail got fuller and fuller, and swung like a pendulum. Occasionally a drop splashed over; but still Tommy Brock snored regularly and never moved,—except one eye.

At last Mr. Tod's preparations were complete. The pail was full of water; the rope was tightly strained over the top of the bed, and across the window-sill to the tree outside.

"It will make a great mess in my bedroom; but I could never

sleep in that bed again without a spring cleaning of some sort," said Mr. Tod.

Mr. Tod took a last look at the badger and softly left the room. He went out of the house, shutting the front door. The rabbits heard his footsteps over the tunnel.

He ran round behind the house, intending to undo the rope in order to let fall the pailful of water upon Tommy Brock—

"I will wake him up with an unpleasant surprise," said Mr. Tod.

The moment he had gone, Tommy Brock got up in a hurry; he rolled Mr. Tod's dressing-gown into a bundle, put it into the bed beneath the pail of water instead of himself, and left the room also—grinning immensely.

He went into the kitchen, lighted the fire and boiled the kettle; for the moment he did not trouble himself to cook the baby rabbits.

When Mr. Tod got to the tree, he found that the weight and strain had dragged the knot so tight that it was past untying. He was obliged to gnaw it with his teeth. He chewed and gnawed for more than twenty minutes. At last the rope gave way with such a sudden jerk that it nearly pulled his teeth out, and quite knocked him over backwards.

Inside the house there was a great crash and splash, and the noise of a pail rolling over and over.

But no screams. Mr. Tod was mystified; he sat quite still, and listened attentively. Then he peeped in at the window. The water was dripping from the bed, the pail had rolled into a corner.

In the middle of the bed under the blanket, was a wet flattened *something*—much dinged in, in the middle where the pail had caught it (as it were across the tummy.) Its head was covered by the wet blanket and it was *not snoring any longer.*

There was nothing stirring, and no sound except the drip, drop, drop drip of water trickling from the mattress.

Mr. Tod watched it for half an hour; his eyes glistened.

Then he cut a caper, and became so bold that he even tapped at the window; but the bundle never moved.

Yes—there was no doubt about it—it had turned out even better than he had planned; the pail had hit poor old Tommy Brock, and killed him dead!

"I will bury that nasty person in the hole which he has dug. I will bring my bedding out, and dry it in the sun," said Mr. Tod.

"I will wash the tablecloth and spread it on the grass in the sun to bleach. And the blanket must be hung up in the wind; and the bed must be thoroughly disinfected, and aired with a warming-pan; and warmed with a hot-water bottle.

"I will get soft soap, and monkey soap, and all sorts of soap; and soda and scrubbing brushes; and persian powder; and carbolic to remove the smell. I must have a disinfecting. Perhaps I may have to burn sulphur."

He hurried round the house to get a shovel from the kitchen— "First I will arrange the hole—then I will drag out that person in the blanket . . . "

He opened the door . . .

Tommy Brock was sitting at Mr. Tod's kitchen table, pouring out tea from Mr. Tod's tea-pot into Mr. Tod's tea-cup. He was quite dry himself and grinning; and he threw the cup of scalding tea all over Mr. Tod.

Then Mr. Tod rushed upon Tommy Brock, and Tommy Brock grappled with Mr. Tod amongst the broken crockery, and there was a terrific battle all over the kitchen. To the rabbits underneath it sounded as if the floor would give way at each crash of falling furniture.

They crept out of their tunnel, and hung about amongst the rocks and bushes, listening anxiously.

Inside the house the racket was fearful.

The rabbit babies in the oven woke up trembling; perhaps it was fortunate they were shut up inside.

Everything was upset except the kitchen table.

And everything was broken, except the mantelpiece and the kitchen fender. The crockery was smashed to atoms.

The chairs were broken, and the window, and the clock fell with a crash, and there were handfuls of Mr. Tod's sandy whiskers.

The vases fell off the mantelpiece, the canisters fell off the shelf; the kettle fell off the hob. Tommy Brock put his foot in a jar of raspberry jam.

And the boiling water out of the kettle fell upon the tail of Mr. Tod.

When the kettle fell, Tommy Brock, who was still grinning, happened to be uppermost; and he rolled Mr. Tod over and over like a log, out at the door.

Then the snarling and worrying went on outside; and they rolled over the bank, and down hill, bumping over the rocks.

There will never be any love lost between Tommy Brock and Mr. Tod.

As soon as the coast was clear, Peter Rabbit and Benjamin Bunny came out of the bushes—

"Now for it! Run in, Cousin Benjamin! Run in and get them! while I watch at the door."

But Benjamin was frightened—

"Oh; oh! they are coming back!"

"No they are not."

"Yes they are!"

"What dreadful bad language! I think they have fallen down the stone quarry."

Still Benjamin hesitated, and Peter kept pushing him—

"Be quick, it's all right. Shut the oven door, Cousin Benjamin, so that he won't miss them."

Decidedly there were lively doings in Mr. Tod's kitchen!

At home in the rabbit hole, things had not been quite comfortable.

After quarrelling at supper, Flopsy and old Mr. Bouncer had passed a sleepless night, and quarrelled again at breakfast. Old Mr. Bouncer could no longer deny that he had invited company into the rabbit hole; but he refused to reply to

the questions and reproaches of Flopsy. The day passed heavily.

Old Mr. Bouncer, very sulky, was huddled up in a corner, barricaded with a chair. Flopsy had taken away his pipe and hidden the tobacco. She had been having a complete turn out and spring-cleaning, to relieve her feelings. She had just finished.

Old Mr. Bouncer, behind his chair, was wondering anxiously what she would do next.

In Mr. Tod's kitchen, amongst the wreckage, Benjamin Bunny picked his way to the oven nervously, through a thick cloud of dust. He opened the oven door, felt inside, and found something warm and wriggling. He lifted it out carefully, and rejoined Peter Rabbit.

"I've got them! Can we get away? Shall we hide, Cousin Peter?"

Peter pricked his ears; distant sounds of fighting still echoed in the wood.

Five minutes afterwards two breathless rabbits came scuttering away down Bull Banks, half carrying, half dragging a sack between them, bumpetty bump over the grass. They reached home safely and burst into the rabbit hole.

Great was old Mr. Bouncer's relief and Flopsy's joy when Peter and Benjamin arrived in triumph with the young family.

The rabbit-babies were rather tumbled and very hungry; they were fed and put to bed. They soon recovered.

A long new pipe and a fresh supply of rabbit tobacco was presented to Mr. Bouncer. He was rather upon his dignity; but he accepted.

Old Mr. Bouncer was forgiven, and they all had dinner. Then Peter and Benjamin told their story—but they had not waited long enough to be able to tell the end of the battle between Tommy Brock and Mr. Tod.

THE END

THE STORY OF
A FIERCE BAD RABBIT

1906

THIS is a fierce bad Rabbit; look at his savage whiskers, and his claws and his turned-up tail.

This is a nice gentle Rabbit. His mother has given him a carrot.

The bad Rabbit would like some carrot.

He doesn't say "Please." He takes it!

And he scratches the
good Rabbit very badly.

The good Rabbit
creeps away, and hides
in a hole. It feels sad.

This is a man with a gun.

He sees something sitting on a bench. He thinks it is a very funny bird!

He comes creeping up behind the trees.

And then he shoots—
BANG!

This is what happens—

But this is all he finds on the bench, when he rushes up with his gun.

The good Rabbit peeps out of its hole.

And it sees the bad Rabbit tearing past— without any tail or whiskers!

THE END